For Phil & Francesca Harrison – RM
To my Family – GM

Text copyright © Roger McGough 2020
Illustrations copyright © Greg McLeod 2020
First published in Great Britain in 2020 and in the USA in 2021 by
Otter-Barry Books, Little Orchard, Burley Gate, Herefordshire, HR1 3QS
www.otterbarrybooks.com

A catalogue record for this book is available from the British Library

ISBN 978-1-91307-497-5
Illustrated with mixed media

Set in DIN Schrift LT
Printed in China

135798642

CROCODILE TEARS

WORDS by ROGER McGOUGH

PICTURES by GREG McLEOD

Otter-Barry BOOKS

The crocodile said to the cockatoo,
"A croc's gotta do
what he's gotta do."

The crocodile said to the chimpanzee,
"Chimpanzee, I want to be free.
The jungle jangle's not for me."

The crocodile said to the mosquito,
"Mosquito, I must quit, oh
I must admit, I just must go."

The crocodile said to the parakeet,
"Parakeet, I'm stifled by this steamy heat.
How I long to loll on a stone-cold street."

The crocodile said to the alligator,
"The Fates await, Alligator, mate.
See you at a later date."

The crocodile said to the hippopotamus,
"Sharon, give my love to Karen,
Gary, Wayne and Darren."

The crocodile said to the piranha,
"Piranha, I leave for London mañana
disguised as a giant banana."

The crocodile said to its mum,
"Mum, the time has come.
I'll write every day, promise."

So, with a rucksack on its back,
it slipped into the stream
and glided miles downriver
to achieve a childhood dream.

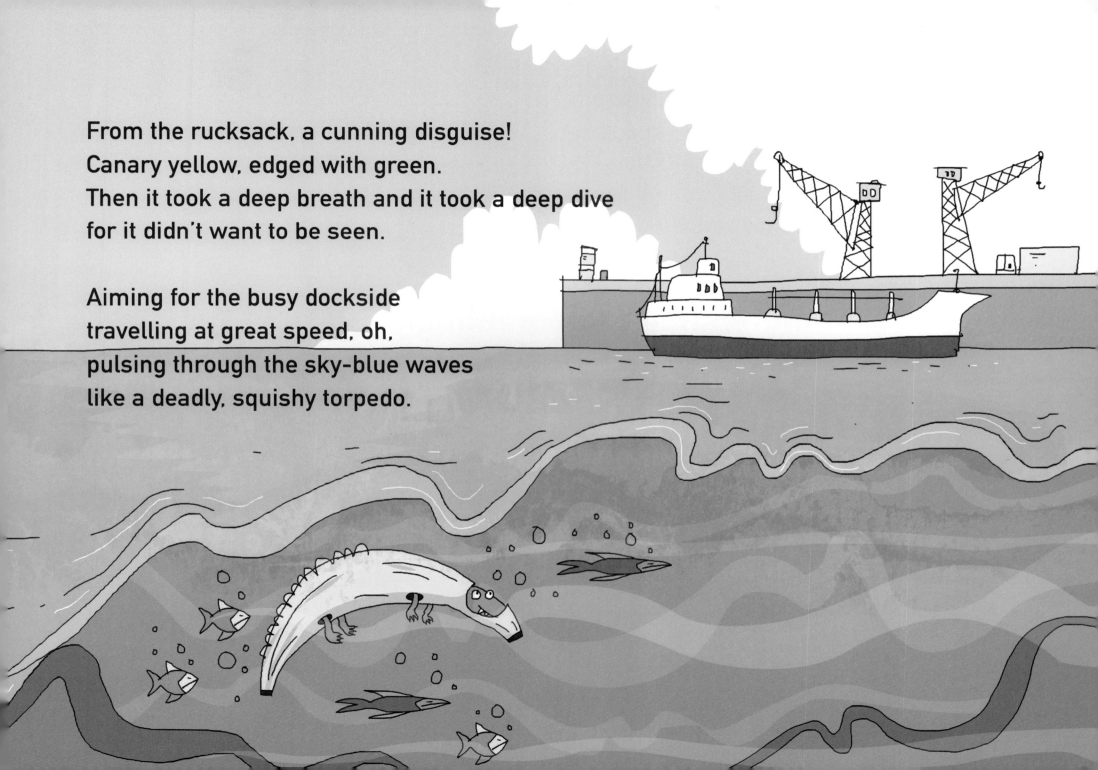

From the rucksack, a cunning disguise!
Canary yellow, edged with green.
Then it took a deep breath and it took a deep dive
for it didn't want to be seen.

Aiming for the busy dockside
travelling at great speed, oh,
pulsing through the sky-blue waves
like a deadly, squishy torpedo.

Then, cheekily, it stowed away
(thanks to the yellowy-green suit)
in the hold of a banana boat,
where it snuggled below with the fruit.

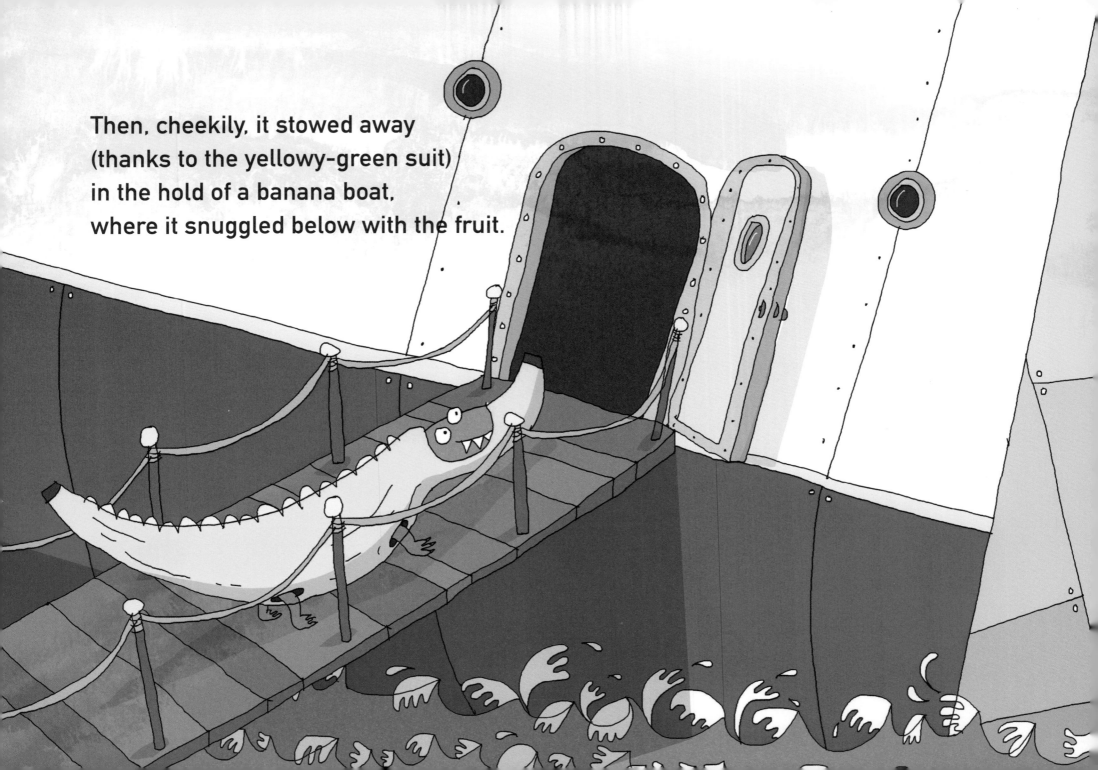

There it slept for most of the voyage,
(for bananas tend to be quiet),
waking occasionally to peel one,
a boring but health-giving diet.

By the banana-skin of its teeth
it disembarked, and with luck
belly-flopped into the back of a van
after a lift on a fork-lift truck.

Early dawn, and the clank of metal
as the van doors open wide
and a crocodile dashes to freedom,
leaving a mush of banana skins inside.

Now crocodiles can go wild in the jungle
but in a city what is there to do?
No fish, no friends, no family
(the plan not really thought through).

Then remembering the promise to Mummy
to write home with news now and then,
the best way to get the ball rolling
was to borrow some paper and a pen.

Dear Mother,

London is grey. The ground is hard.
Buildings are giants with their heads in the clouds.

The fiercest animals are called cars.
They screech and scream, trailing bad breath.

Humans rush by, shouting into their hands
as if time was on fire.

I lie low. Keep to the gutter
where I can slidder undisturbed.

Dear Mother,

Buses are red elephants,
stampeding and trumpeting.

Dogs pull humans to parks
where they are let off the leash.

Rats abound. Though kept in prisons
underground, they escape at will.

Birds are not feathered rainbows
but the colour of worn pavements.

Too busy squibbling over crumbs,
they have no time to sing.

Dear Mother,

During daylight, sightsee.
See sights for sore eyes.

See eyesores soar into the sky.
So far have sightseen the Shard,

the Gherkin, the Walkie Talkie,
the Slab and the Pointy Thing.

Yesterday I went to Madame Tussaud's
and ate lots of famous people.

Dear Mother,

Moonlight becomes crocodile.
Midnight after rain is my favourite time.

In a quiet street away from the city centre
I wait patiently. Still and silent as a puddle.

Befuddled reveller returning home late
beware the puddle that moves.

Beware the reflection that salivates.
Moonlight that becomes crocodile.

Dear Mother,

Snow in London. The ground is cold.
Ice in my bones, I'm feeling old.

Too tired to hunt, I eat pizza boxes,
coke cans, fried chicken buckets.

How best to describe the way I feel?
The crocodile tears I shed

are not crocodile tears.
They are real.

Dear Mother,

My stomach was empty, I'd had my fill
of city life, it made me ill.

The time had come to go away,
to find a ship and stow away.

So here I lie among the cargo
of a steamer bound for Santiago.

And when I smell my jungle, the trees and the sand
I'll slip overboard and strike out for land.

"Chimpanzee and Cockatoo,
how I've missed my jungle crew.
Mosquito and Parakeet,
the tales I'll tell when next we meet.

Piranha and Alligator,
I felt a bump as we crossed the equator.
Sharon and the gang, I'm on my way.
See you soon. Hip hippo hooray!"

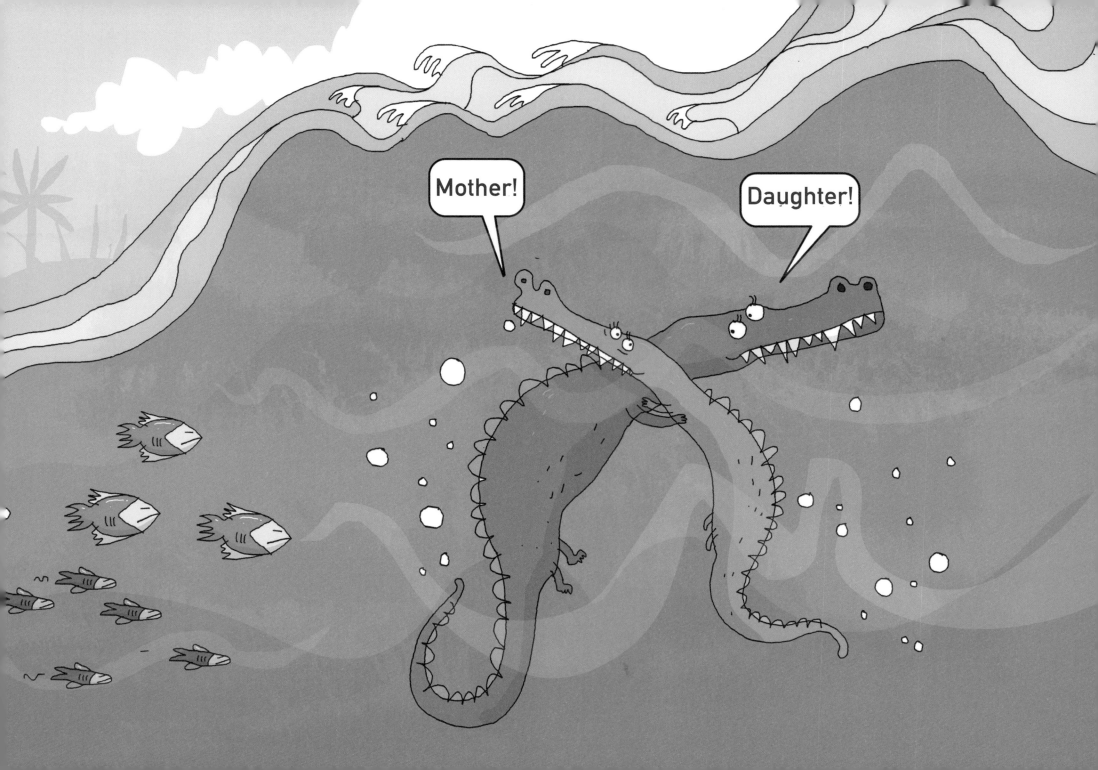

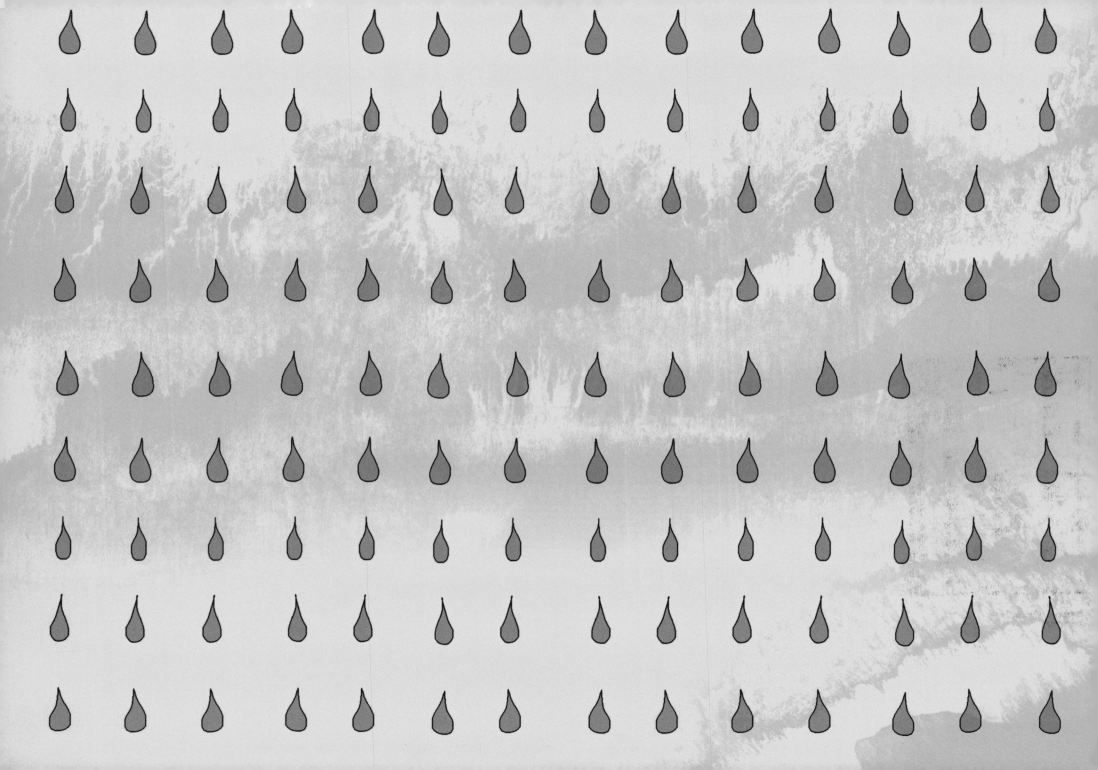